RAINY DAY!

Patricia Lakin

pictures by
Scott Nash

DIAL BOOKS FOR YOUNG READERS

For Scott Nash and Nancy Gibson-Nash,
two talented and generous artists
–P. L.

To Kirsten & Curious City
Where Kids and Books Meet
–S. N.

With thanks to Scott Whitehouse for his Photoshop design work. –S.N.

DIAL BOOKS FOR YOUNG READERS
A division of Penguin Young Readers Group
Published by The Penguin Group
Penguin Group (USA) Inc., 375 Hudson Street,
New York, NY 10014, U.S.A.
Penguin Group (Canada), 90 Eglinton Avenue East,
Suite 700, Toronto, Ontario, Canada M4P 2Y3 (a division of Pearson Penguin Canada Inc.)
Penguin Books Ltd, 80 Strand, London WC2R 0RL, England
Penguin Ireland, 25 St. Stephen's Green, Dublin 2,
Ireland (a division of Penguin Books Ltd)
Penguin Group (Australia), 250 Camberwell Road, Camberwell,
Victoria 3124, Australia (a division of Pearson Australia Group Pty Ltd)
Penguin Books India Pvt Ltd, 11 Community Centre, Panchsheel Park,
New Delhi - 110 017, India
Penguin Group (NZ), Cnr Airborne and Rosedale Roads, Albany, Auckland 1310,
New Zealand (a division of Pearson New Zealand Ltd)
Penguin Books (South Africa) (Pty) Ltd, 24 Sturdee Avenue, Rosebank, Johannesburg 2196, South Africa
Penguin Books Ltd, Registered Offices: 80 Strand, London WC2R 0RL, England
Text copyright © 2007 by Patricia Lakin
Pictures copyright © 2007 by Scott Nash

The publisher does not have any control over and does not
assume any responsibility for author or third-party websites or their content.
Text set in Futura
Manufactured in China on acid-free paper

1   3   5   7   9   10   8   6   4   2

Library of Congress Cataloging-in-Publication Data
Lakin, Patricia, date.
Rainy day! / Patricia Lakin ; pictures by Scott Nash.
p.   cm.
Summary: Four crocodiles find all sorts of ways to keep busy on a rainy day.
ISBN 978-0-8037-3092-2
[1. Play—Fiction. 2. Rain and rainfall—Fiction. 3. Books and reading—Fiction. 4. Crocodiles—Fiction.
5. Stories in rhyme.] I. Nash, Scott, date, ill. II. Title.
PZ8.3.L26Rai 2007
[E]—dc22
2005025367

The art was produced in black Prismacolor pencil and Photoshop..

"Not another rainy day!"
cried Sam, Pam, Will and Jill.

Nothing to make.

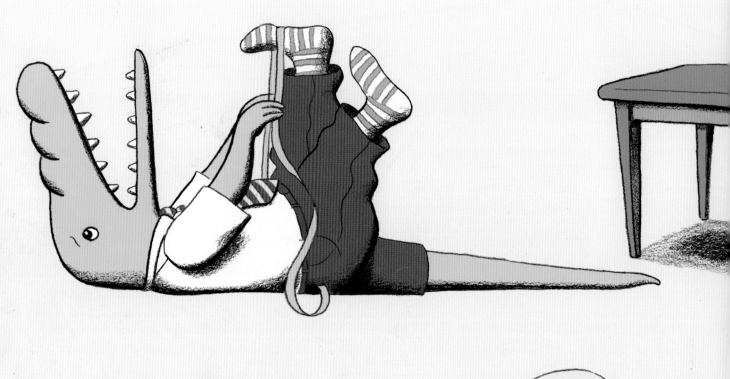

Nothing to bake.

Nothing to paint.

Nothing to play.

"LET'S GO OUT

SIDE ANYWAY!"

"Umbrellas," said Sam.

"Rain coats," said Pam.

"Rain boots," said Will.

"Rain hats," said Jill.

"READY!"

said Sam, Pam, Will and Jill.

The road got wet.

The fog got thick.

They didn't know which road to pick.

They took a left.

They took a right.

A pirate ship came into sight.

Then a whale

and a monster face!

Just what was this scary place?

"A mini-golf park!"

cheered Sam, Pam, Will and Jill.

"LET'S PLAY!"

"Smack it!"
said Sam.

"Putt it!"
said Pam.

"Hit it!"
said Will.

"Lost it!" said Jill.

"FORGET IT!"
said Sam, Pam, Will and Jill.

GRRRRR!

"Who's there?"
cried Sam.

"A bear!"
cried Pam.

"Wild hog!"
cried Will.

"A dog!"
cried Jill.

"With a BASEBALL,"
cried Sam, Pam, Will and Jill.

"LINE UP,"

said Sam.

"POP UP!"
said Sam, Pam, Will and Jill.

"GOT IT!"
said Sam.

"GOT IT!"
said Pam.

"GOT IT!"
said Will.

"NOT IT!"
said Jill.

"HAIL!"

said Sam, Pam, Will and Jill.

"I'm slipping!" cried Sam.

"I'm sliding!" cried Pam.

"I'm soaking!" cried Will.

"I'm sinking!" cried Jill.

"NOW WHAT?"
cried Sam, Pam, Will, and Jill.

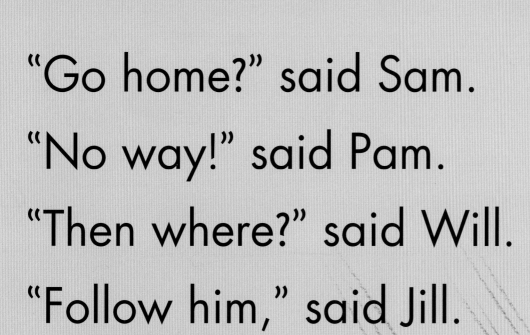

"Go home?" said Sam.

"No way!" said Pam.

"Then where?" said Will.

"Follow him," said Jill.

"To the library!"
said Sam, Pam, Will and Jill.

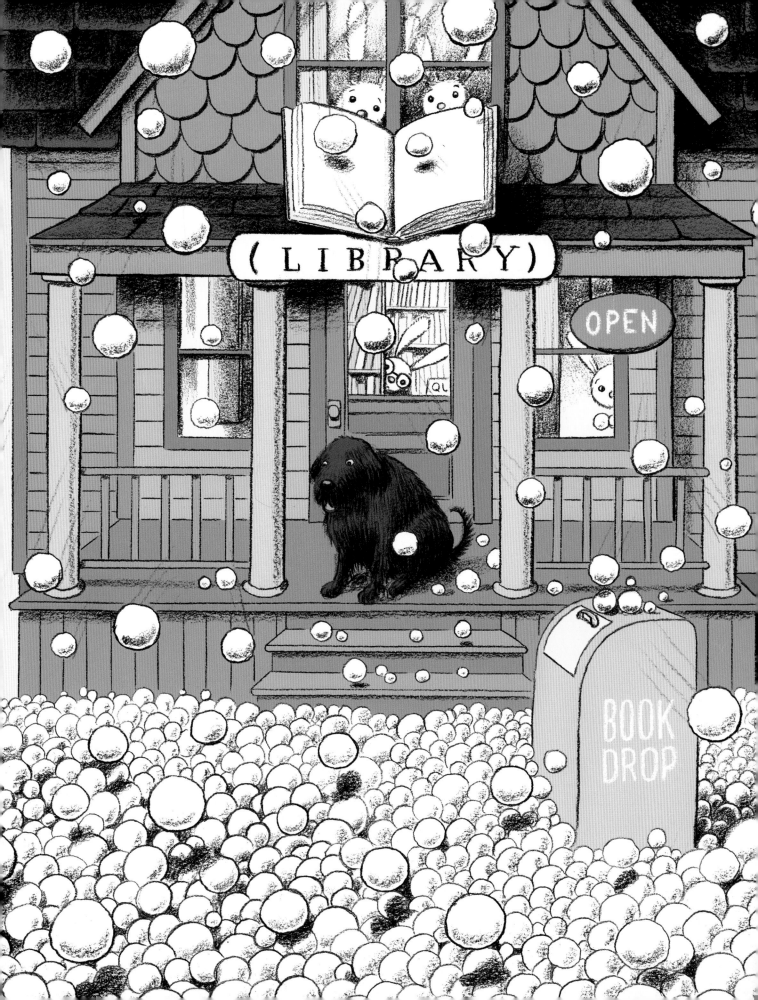

They each took a look.
They each took a book.
They each took a nook.

"Pirates," said Sam.

"Golf," said Pam.

"Perfect!"

sighed Sam, Pam, Will and Jill.